The Gryphon Press

—a voice for the voiceless—

To those who foster compassion toward all animals

—Juanita Havill

The author is grateful to the following people for their generosity in sharing their knowledge, experience, and expertise with her: Barbara Columbo, Animal Humane Society, Minneapolis, MN; Lesley Esselburn, Executive Director, TROT, Tucson, AZ; Mary-Louise Gould, Epona Senior Faculty Member at EponaQuest, LLC, Sonoita, AZ; Catherine Huddleston, Director/Lead Trainer Equine Division of Challenge-U, Fallbrook, CA; Jean Jay, Director of Communications, Missouri Humane Society, St. Louis, MO; Ann Jost, Founder and President, Care for the Horses, Inc., Sierra Vista, AZ; Karen Pomroy, Founder/Director, Equine Voices Rescue & Sanctuary, Green Valley, AZ; Mary Vardi, Director of Instruction, TROT, Tucson, AZ; Julia H. Wilson, DVM, Diplomate, ACVIM, Associate Professor, Large Animal Medicine, Veterinary Population Medicine, College of Veterinary Medicine, St. Paul, MN.

Printed in Canada by Friesens Corporation
Text set in Book Antiqua by BookMobile Design and Publishing Services,
Minneapolis, Minnesota

Library of Congress Control Number: 2009932446
ISBN: 978-0-940719-10-1
3 5 7 9 10 8 6 4 2
A portion of profits from this book will be
donated to shelters and animal rescue societies.

I am the voice of the voiceless:
Through me, the dumb shall speak;
Till the deaf world's ear be made to hear
The cry of the wordless weak.

—from a poem by Ella Wheeler Wilcox, early 20th-century poet

Call the Horse LUCKY

Juanita Havill · Nancy Lane

Mel saw the horse first. "Look, Gramma, a pinto. We didn't see a horse out here last fall."

Gramma shook her head. "And I haven't ridden here since then."

"He's all alone." Mel wanted the horse to look up or maybe even to trot toward them, but he didn't move.

On the ride back to Gramma's house, Mel said, "I wish I could have a horse."

That night Mel dreamed about the pinto in the corral on the country road.

The next day Mel rode back to the corral with carrots in her pocket. "Hey, boy," Mel called.

The horse didn't raise his head.

Eyes half-closed, he stood like a skinny statue with a bony back and ribs that stuck out. He didn't swish his tail or shake his head to flick off the swarm of flies crawling on his rump, legs, and face. Mounds of smelly muck lay around him.

Mel waved a carrot. The horse closed his eyes as if to gain strength. Slowly he shuffled toward the fence. It hurt Mel to watch him move. Maybe she shouldn't have brought the carrots. But she held one out and waited.

After a while, the horse took the carrot. While he chewed, Mel reached out to touch his face. His red-rimmed eyes looked sunken. Mel knew something was very wrong.

Mel blinked back tears when she described the horse to Gramma. "We have to help him."

After Gramma called the Humane Society, she told Mel, "Sooner or later they will rescue the horse—sooner if the owner gives up the horse, and later if the owner is taken to court."

Mel and Gramma rode out every day to see if the horse was still there. One afternoon they saw people in the corral with the horse.

Mel called out, "Did you come to help the horse?"

"We're taking him to Lisa's ranch, where he can get well," said a man in a blue uniform.

"I'm Lisa," the woman said. "I run the horse rescue ranch. I'm afraid this little gelding has gone hungry for a long time. We persuaded the owner to give him up. I'm glad that someone told the Humane Society about him."

"Gramma did," said Mel.

"Because of Mel," said Gramma.

"He'll get better, won't he?" Mel asked.

"I think so," said Lisa. "A vet will treat him and we'll feed and care for him. Don't you think he needs a name, Mel?"

"Let's call him Lucky," Mel said. "I want him to have lots of luck."

Mel felt better when they drove up to the rescue ranch a few weeks later. It looked like a place where horses could be happy.

"Is that Lucky?" Mel shouted. "His fly mask sort of hides his eyes. He's not so skinny anymore. And he has a friend."

"Flicker showed interest in Lucky as soon as he arrived," Lisa said.

"At first we kept Lucky alone while he got better," she said. "Then we put him in a pasture with Flicker, and they get along fine. Horses are herd animals. They don't like to be alone, but sometimes socializing with a bunch of strangers is hard on a horse that isn't well. And the other horses might bully him."

"He likes to be brushed, doesn't he?"

"From the beginning, Lucky let us handle and groom him. Not all rescued horses will let you, but Lucky was pretty calm even though he had pain from his infected hoof."

"He had trouble walking," said Mel. "Did you give him medicine?"

“Yes, and his hoof has healed.” Lisa told Mel that when Lucky came, the vet gave him a thorough examination.

"Then Lucky had to be wormed, his hooves attended to, and his teeth cared for. He seemed to know we were here to help him. I hope he finds a good home."

Mel read the adoption questionnaire and thought, *We don't have enough room for Lucky at my house. The backyard is too tiny, and Gramma doesn't even have a yard.*

"Lucky, why do you cost so much to take care of?" she said to the pinto.

She didn't know how she could ever own him, but at least for now she could see him.

A month later Lucky went to live and work at a horse therapy ranch. Gramma drove Mel to see Lucky.

The trainer invited them to watch her work with Lucky.

She stood in a round pen with Lucky and rubbed him with a wadded plastic bag. Then she opened the bag and waved it. Lucky stood still.

"Good boy," said the trainer. "Like most horses, Lucky was startled at first when I shook a plastic bag near him."

After Lucky circled the pen for a while, the trainer hooked the lead to his halter. "Would you like to lead him back to the pasture?"

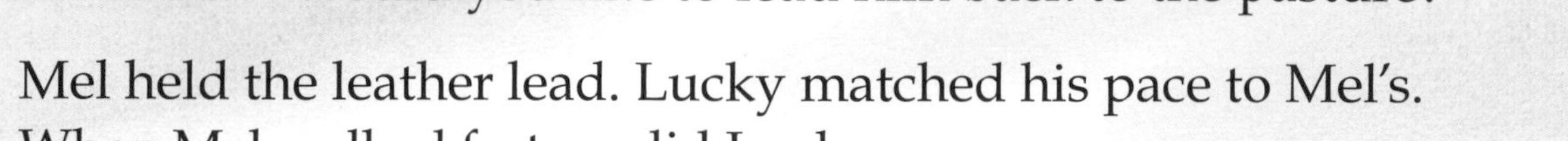

Mel held the leather lead. Lucky matched his pace to Mel's.
When Mel walked fast, so did Lucky.
When Mel slowed down, Lucky did, too.

"You lead him well," said the trainer.
"Have you thought of volunteering to work here?
We need people to groom and walk the horses."

Mel turned to Gramma.
"When I visit you, I can be with Lucky."

"It's a wonderful idea," Gramma said.

"My name should be Lucky, too." Mel reached up to stroke Lucky's neck. "I'm lucky to have found you."

Helping Horses Like Lucky

Horse neglect and abuse: It is a sad fact that each year over a thousand horses are neglected or abused in the U.S. Many factors contribute to horse neglect, including:

- difficult economic times
- weather-related increases in the price of hay
- job loss or unexpected demands on the horse owner's finances.

Unable to keep their horses, many people turn them over to animal welfare organizations. Abusive or neglectful owners who do not surrender their horses can be forced by court order to give up their horses. Horse neglect and abuse are crimes, punishable by fines and jail time.

Horse rescue ranches: Facilities for neglected and abused horses exist in many states. Responsible rescue ranches provide medical care and pay careful attention to the animals' diet. Not all horses recover, especially those with severe infections and long-term malnutrition, and they are humanely euthanized. Others recover and can be adopted. Some horse rescue ranches prefer a foster system in which people accept the responsibility of caring for the horses while ownership remains with the rescue facility.

Horse adoption: Anyone who plans to adopt a horse should ask:

- Can I afford the cost of food, medical care, boarding, and supplies for the horse?
- Do I have experience from previous horse ownership?
- Do I have adequate space and shelter for a horse?
- Will I be able to spend time with my horse?

Horse therapy facilities: Horse therapy, also called hippotherapy, serves children and adults with injuries or diseases that limit their physical mobility, such as cerebral palsy. Horseback riding enables these individuals to experience movement. Interacting with horses has also been shown to benefit children and adults with emotional or psychological problems, such as autism, attention deficit disorder, depression, or low self-esteem. Therapy horses must be gentle, reliable, and calm. Because of their traumatic backgrounds, neglected and abused horses are not generally good candidates for horseback-riding therapy.

How you can help:

- Report gaunt, starved-looking horses or horses with untreated injuries to your local law enforcement agency, humane society, or animal welfare agency.
- If you have to give up your horse, contact your veterinarian, farrier, or other local horse owners to try to find a suitable home for your horse. Rescue ranches often focus on the neediest cases.
- Donate funds to a rescue ranch in which you have confidence.
- Support legislation that promotes humane treatment of horses.
- Volunteer at a horse rescue or therapy ranch where you will interact with horses on a regular basis. (If you are considering horse ownership, spending time with horses is excellent preparation.)

The following organizations maintain Web sites with information about horse neglect, rescue, and therapy:

- American Hippotherapy Association: *www.americanhippotherapyassociation.org*
- American Society for the Prevention of Cruelty to Animals: *www.aspca.org*
- The Humane Society of the United States: *www.humanesociety.org*
- North American Riding for the Handicapped Association: *www.narha.org*
- United States Equine Rescue League, Inc.: *www.userl.org*